Adapted by Ellie O'Ryan

Based on the series created by Dan Povenmire & Jeff "Swampy" Marsh

DISNEY PRESS

New York

Part ONE

Lawrence Fletcher hummed as he walked out of the garage. It was an extremely hot day, and he was loading the family car with piles of boxes. He paused at the fence along the driveway to glance into the backyard, where his sons, Phineas and Ferb, were standing on their heads.

"So, what are you boys thinking of doing today?" he asked.

"We don't know," Phineas groaned, still upside down. "It's too hot to think!"

For anyone who knew Phineas and Ferb, this was huge news. Ever since summer had started, the boys—who were stepbrothers *and* best friends—had vowed to make every day count. They didn't want to waste a moment of their summer freedom, not when they could have all sorts of exciting adventures. But today was already turning into one of the hottest days on record, and it threatened to derail their goal of an entire summer filled with fun. If all Phineas and Ferb could think of doing was standing on their heads, something was wrong! The boys' pet platypus, Perry, stood by listlessly. He didn't even have the energy to make his funny chittering noise.

"Yeah," their father said sympathetically. "Mom and I are getting rid of a few old things at the antiques store, but I think I've got just what you need!" Their father disappeared into the garage. When he came back out, he was carrying a folding table and a strange green machine that had a crank on one side. "It's a snow-cone machine, just like when I was a kid!" he said excitedly.

"How does it work?" Phineas asked as he and Ferb approached the table.

Mr. Fletcher was happy to demonstrate. "Well, you pour ice in here, you give it a crank,

add some syrup, and Bob's your uncle—snow cones for everyone!"

The boys' father proudly handed two snow cones to Phineas and Ferb. The slushy ice was drenched with delicious blue syrup. It was the perfect refreshing treat for a hot day.

Just then, the boys' mom, Linda, honked the car horn. "Honey, we need to go!" she called from the driveway. "The antiques show closes in just twelve hours!"

"Okay, kids," Mr. Fletcher said to his sons, "I'll leave you in charge of the machine." He glanced back at the house, where the boys' older sister, Candace, was. "And be easy on your sister," he added. "She's been a bit on edge lately."

As their parents drove away, Phineas licked his snow cone. "Wow, snow in July," he marveled. Those four little words gave him an idea. "That's it! I know what we're gonna do today!" he exclaimed. He looked down at his snow cone. "We're going to need a lot more ice."

But before Phineas and Ferb could get to work, Candace stormed into the yard. She had dedicated her summer to busting her brothers' outrageous plans. There was just one problem. Their crazy inventions always seemed to disappear right before Mom showed up!

"What is all this?" Candace yelled.

"It's a snow cone. You want some?" Phineas

asked, holding up the treat so that Candace could have a taste.

"You mean crushed ice covered with blue carbs?" Candace scoffed. "Lame!" Then she stalked off to the house, where she could hide out in her air-conditioned room.

"Maybe Perry wants some," Phineas said as Ferb started cranking the handle on the snow-cone machine, making a mound of shaved ice.

But when the brothers looked around, they didn't see their pet anywhere. "Hey, where's Perry?" Phineas asked.

What the boys didn't know was that Perry

was no ordinary platypus. He was actually a top secret agent for a group called Organization Without a Cool Acronym, or O.W.C.A. for short. Agent P, as he was known, lived a double life. His identity as a friendly pet platypus was just a cover to keep him safe. In reality, he was dedicated to a life of fighting crime!

In all the excitement over the snow-cone machine, Agent P had seen the perfect opportunity to slip away to his underground lair. He slapped his ultracool fedora onto his head and jumped into the coils of an ordinary-looking garden hose. Then he carefully twisted the faucet just the right way to open a hidden tunnel which led straight to his lair.

Whoosh! Agent P zipped through the tunnel and did an impressive midair somersault before landing in a comfy captain's chair. Facing a large flat-screen monitor, Agent P was ready to receive his latest mission briefing from Major Monogram, the commander of the O.W.C.A.

"Good morning, Agent P," Major Monogram said in his gruff voice. "I'll get right to it. This time, we're worried about Dr. Doofenshmirtz buying laser pointers. I mean, two or three of them would be fine, but he just put in an order for eighteen thousand of them! Only a crazed, evil, and diabolical mind would do that! I'm sure you'll know what to do, Agent P."

The secret-agent platypus saluted, then jumped out of his chair and started to run. Dr. Doofenshmirtz, the self-proclaimed evil genius of Danville, had been Agent P's nemesis for a long time now. Again and again, Agent P had managed to thwart even his most fiendish schemes. But that wasn't going to stop the evil doctor from pursuing his lifelong goal of taking over the Tri-State Area.

And Agent P knew better than to relax when Dr. Doofenshmirtz was working on a devious new plot. The fate of the Tri-State Area depended on him!

Chapter TWO

Back at Phineas and Ferb's house, the brothers were hard at work. And the little snow-cone machine was working overtime! Phineas and Ferb had filled their backyard with rotating electric fans and portable air-conditioning units to prevent the snow from melting. Using his mechanical expertise, Ferb had attached a powerful motor to the snow-cone machine to keep its handle cranking.

Soon, the boys' backyard was filled with fluffy, frosty ice crystals that seemed just like real snowflakes.

"Hey, Phineas!" a girl called as she walked into the yard. It was Isabella Garcia-Shapiro, one of the brothers' best friends.

"Hi, Isabella," Phineas replied.

"What'cha doin'?" asked Isabella.

"We're making s'winter!" Phineas said excitedly, pointing to the snow that was accumulating all over the backyard.

"'S'winter'?" Isabella asked in confusion.

"It's a unique and logic-defying amalgam of winter and summer," Ferb quietly explained in his British accent.

"Why have snow in the winter when it's too cold to enjoy it?" added Phineas.

Isabella's eyes lit up. Everybody knew that when Phineas and Ferb got started on their daily activity, an awesome adventure was about to begin—and she couldn't wait to be part of it!

"You guys are gonna need some help," she said. Isabella whistled loudly. Instantly, four Fireside Girls appeared, carrying shovels and skis.

Phineas grinned at the new arrivals. With the Fireside Girls there to help, making a mountain of snow on the hottest day of summer was going to be easier than he had thought!

Meanwhile, in her bedroom, Candace was chatting with her best friend, Stacy, on the phone. "I think cheerleaders are overrated anyway," Candace complained. "I mean, being gorgeous and popular. Does that matter in the real world?"

But as she talked, her room suddenly grew darker and darker. Candace looked over to her window and realized something was blocking the light. "What is going on out there?" she asked.

Candace dropped her phone and rushed over to the window. She tried to open it, but it wouldn't budge.

"*Ugh—argh—urgh!*" Candace grunted as she used all her strength to push it open.

Suddenly, an avalanche of snow poured into her bedroom! Candace clawed her way outside. She stared in shock at the snow-covered mountain that now towered over her house.

"Phineas!" Candace yelled. "What's going on here?"

"It's summer and winter together," Phineas called back. "It's s'winter!"

Phineas was right. The Flynn-Fletcher backyard was packed with kids enjoying the world's best snow day—all under a blazing summer sun! Some kids were ice-skating, and some were sledding. Others were having snowball fights or making snow angels. A few kids were skiing, and one was going for a ride in a horse-drawn sleigh. There was even a snowman relaxing on a lounge chair, working on his tan!

"Some people call it wummer," Phineas added helpfully.

Candace narrowed her eyes as she held up her cell phone. "I'm calling Mom, you know," she said.

But as she was dialing, something happened that made her pause. Out of the corner of her eye, Candace caught a glimpse of a tall, gorgeous guy walking past her window.

It was her crush, Jeremy!

"Jeremy?" she asked in surprise.

"Hey, Candace!" Jeremy said in a friendly voice. "Do you want to go skiing?"

"I'd love to," Candace began, "but—but I am so afraid of heights."

Jeremy's face fell. "Bummer," he replied. "Well, see you later then."

Jeremy turned away and headed back up the snow mountain. Then Candace heard him call out, "Hey, D.D., wait up!" She watched in horror as Jeremy jumped onto the ski lift next to somebody with long, blond hair—a person Candace had never seen before.

"D.D.?" Candace gasped as she called Stacy back. "Stacy, who's D.D.?"

Stacy replied on the other end.

"A Swedish exchange student?" Candace cried. "I gotta go!"

Candace dropped her phone and leaped out the window, still wearing her favorite white skirt and red tank top even though she was now knee-deep in snow.

"Hey, wait for me!" she called after Jeremy. She shoved her way through the line to the ski lift.

A few moments later, Candace grabbed a seat right behind Jeremy and D.D. To Candace's left sat a tall, dark-haired girl. It was Vanessa Doofenshmirtz, Dr. Doofenshmirtz's daughter.

"My brothers are just driving me crazy!" Candace complained to Vanessa.

"You should try spending an hour with my dad sometime," Vanessa replied.

But Candace didn't respond. At that moment, she looked down and realized just how high the ski lift was going! "*Aaaah!*" she screamed. "I had no idea this thing was so high!" In a complete panic, Candace grabbed the long straps from her seat belt and tied them into a triple knot, right over the buckle. "There," she said, breathing a sigh of relief. With a knot like that, Candace figured it would be impossible for her to fall off the ski lift as it soared through the air.

When the ski lift reached the top of the mountain, Jeremy and D.D. hopped off. Then it was Candace's and Vanessa's turn to jump down. Candace took a deep breath.

"Great," she said, trying to sound confident. "Here we go!"

Candace fumbled with the knot, but before she could get her seat belt undone, the ski lift turned around and started flying back down the mountain! "Wait, wait, *wait!*" she cried.

But it was hopeless. The ski lift whisked Candace right back to the bottom. Now she'd have to find the courage to get back up to the top again.

But this time, she was going to skip the lift!

Chapter
THREE

Inside his evil lair, Dr. Doofenshmirtz rubbed his hands gleefully as he thought of the recent renovations he'd made to the entrance of Doofenshmirtz Evil, Incorporated. Neon signs flashed: DOOFENSHMIRTZ SECRET HIDEOUT and DO NOT ENTER, while an icon of a platypus with a thick red line slashed across it was attached to the door. Dr. Doofenshmirtz was sure that Perry the Platypus wouldn't be able

23

to resist bursting into the lair—through the *front* door—when he saw all those fancy signs warning him to keep out.

And right on the other side of the door, a large red X marked the spot where Agent P would meet his doom! It was the perfect trap, really—so simple that it had taken a stroke of genius to dream it up.

"As soon as he walks through that front door, no more Perry the Platypus!" Dr. Doofenshmirtz cackled to himself as ominous piano music swelled. But the piano music wasn't echoing from a well-timed sound track. It was coming from the most essential part of the trap itself: a baby grand piano that hovered dangerously overhead, ready to plunge to the floor as soon as Agent P stepped onto the X!

"It's genius, right?" Dr. Doofenshmirtz asked the man playing the piano. Then he got a funny feeling that someone was standing behind him. He spun around to look—and found himself face-to-face with Agent P!

"Oh! Oh, I told Nancy to keep the back door locked!" Dr. Doofenshmirtz exclaimed in outrage when he realized that Agent P had managed to avoid the trap. Then he cleared his throat and pulled a small tape recorder out of his pocket. "Note to self: my evil deed for tomorrow—fire the maid."

"What are you looking at?" Dr. Doofenshmirtz snapped at Agent P. Suddenly, the secret-agent platypus whipped out a grappling-hook gun.

"Not so fast, Perry the Platypus!" Dr. Doofenshmirtz cried, yanking a secret lever.

Splurt!

A thick, gooey, brown liquid splattered all over Agent P!

"Don't worry, it's not what you think," Dr. Doofenshmirtz assured him. "It's my special recipe for quick-hardening chocolate!"

Agent P didn't say anything. He didn't even move. He couldn't—because the chocolate had already hardened around him, forming a trap!

Dr. Doofenshmirtz smiled evilly. Now he could tell Agent P all about his latest diabolical scheme. And there was nothing the platypus could do to stop him!

"Between you and me, my popularity has plummeted to an all-time low," Dr. Doofenshmirtz began to explain. He unrolled a large graph with labels such as LOW, LOWER,

and OUCH, to show Agent P what he was talking about. One glance at the chart and it was clear that Dr. Doofenshmirtz's popularity levels really were in the toilet. But Agent P couldn't see it. He was still stuck in the chocolate!

"But everybody loves chocolate!" Dr. Doofenshmirtz said. "What if I could re-create chocolate in my own image? Behold, the Melt-inator 6-5000, powered by thousands of laser pointers!"

With a flourish, Dr. Doofenshmirtz pushed a button to unveil his latest invention. The Melt-inator 6-5000 rose all the way up through the ceiling. It was an enormous contraption that held eighteen thousand laser pointers and aimed them through a powerful magnifying glass.

"It has a melting capacity of seven!" Dr. Doofenshmirtz bragged. "That's on a scale of one to five, so it's a big number! Here, watch this!"

Dr. Doofenshmirtz played a video that showed the Melt-inator 6-5000 blasting its laser beam at a chocolate shop. In the video, all the delicious chocolate melted into a river of goo that flowed right into a gutter. It ran along the underground sewer tunnels until it reached Doofenshmirtz Evil, Incorporated, where it was poured into special molds shaped like Dr. Doofenshmirtz himself. The devious doctor was planning to steal all the Tri-State Area's chocolate to create mini edible statues that looked like him! Since everyone loved chocolate, Dr. Doofenshmirtz was sure these treats would make his popularity levels skyrocket!

"Now, do you understand what you're up against?" Dr. Doofenshmirtz laughed maniacally.

But Agent P did not respond.

"Come on, you didn't get any of that?" Dr. Doofenshmirtz asked, frustrated. "You didn't get *any* of that?" He sighed. "Oh, okay. I will start again. First, my popularity is at an all-time low. You got that, right?"

Dr. Doofenshmirtz didn't care if he had to explain his diabolical plot to Agent P twice, or ten times, or a *hundred* times. It would be worth it to make sure the platypus truly understood just how evil he could be!

Chapter
FOUR

Back at the Flynn-Fletcher house, the sun was still shining and the snow was still falling. And Candace was still trying to figure out a way to get back up the mountain.

"All right," she said as she tied a pair of tennis rackets to her feet. With these makeshift snowshoes, she'd be able to get to the

31

top for sure. "Nothing will stand in my way!" she said determinedly.

But as she started to walk, Candace sank deeper and deeper into the snow. Soon, she was completely buried. A dogsled even *whooshed* right over her.

Candace groaned as she dug her way out. But then, she had a great idea. "Wait a minute," Candace said, eyeing the dogsled. "I got it!"

All Candace needed was her very own sled pulled by the neighborhood bully, Buford.

Then she could easily make it to the top of the mountain . . . in style!

Meanwhile, at Doofenshmirtz Evil, Incorporated, Dr. Doofenshmirtz had given up on explaining his devious plan to Agent P. Instead, he would let the secret agent see it with his own two eyes!

The doctor crossed the room to the Melt-inator 6-5000 and pulled a lever. The contraption began to rise high into the air and up through the ceiling. As he fiddled with the control panel, an image of the World's Largest Chocolate Bar appeared on the screen.

"At this very moment, the World's Largest Chocolate Bar is passing through town on its way to the Smithsonian—but it will never arrive!" Dr. Doofenshmirtz declared. His finger hovered above the large orange button that would activate the Melt-inator 6-5000. "In five . . . four . . . three . . ." He glanced over at Agent P, who was still a motionless chocolate statue. "Two and a half, two and a quarter," Dr. Doofenshmirtz said slowly.

Then he paused and walked over to Agent P. "Is that it? Is that—? You're not going to do anything? You're just going to stand there like a dead fish? I'm giving you a chance to

do something here!" he exclaimed.

But chocolate-statue Agent P didn't reply.

Dr. Doofenshmirtz sighed. "This used to be more fun," he grumbled as he resumed his countdown. "One and a half . . . one and a quarter." He couldn't stand being ignored. "You know, in some cultures it's considered rude not to—"

Wham!

Out of nowhere, Agent P flew up behind Dr. Doofenshmirtz and gave him a well-aimed karate kick to the back of his head! The blow knocked the doctor halfway across the lab. He finally skidded to a stop right next to Agent P's chocolate statue.

"Perry the Platypus!" he cried. "But how did you . . . ?" Then, Dr. Doofenshmirtz noticed that a hole had been chewed out of the chocolate statue's backside!

"You ate your own *heinie*?" Dr. Doofenshmirtz gasped in disbelief.

He scrambled up and raced over to the Melt-inator 6-5000's controls. "I must aim it! Quickly!"

He used all his strength to turn the large wheel that would aim the Melt-inator 6-5000 at the World's Largest Chocolate Bar.

But Agent P was ready. The resourceful platypus yanked a lever that sent the wheel spinning so fast Dr. Doofenshmirtz couldn't keep up. It bopped the doctor on the chin and spun him right across the room! Thanks to Agent P's interference, the World's Largest Chocolate Bar was safe . . . for now. But outside, the Melt-inator 6-5000 was still spinning wildly, aiming at houses, businesses . . . and even Phineas and Ferb's parents, who were driving home in their car!

Mr. and Mrs. Flynn-Fletcher had no idea they were in the crosshairs of the Melt-inator 6-5000 as they drove along in the family station wagon. The car was loaded down with all sorts of antiques and oddities. A giant cuckoo clock was strapped to the roof of the car.

"Oh, the kids are gonna love this Austrian-style cuckoo clock," Phineas and Ferb's dad said enthusiastically.

Suddenly, the car was enveloped in a bright flash of red light. Both parents cried out as the vehicle started bumping awkwardly along the road.

"Maybe we should pull over and see what's going on," Mr. Fletcher said. They stopped the car on the side of the road and climbed out. To their surprise, all four of the car's tires were

flat and smoking. It almost looked as if they had melted!

"That's peculiar," Mr. Fletcher said thoughtfully.

"Good thing we also bought those four spare tires, huh?" his wife added cheerfully.

As they changed the tires, Phineas and Ferb's parents had no idea how close they had come to being hit by a blast from the Meltinator 6-5000.

They also had no way of knowing that their backyard had been turned into a snowy winter wonderland!

Back at home, Candace was smiling.
"Thanks!" she cried as Buford finished pulling
her to the top of the
snowy mountain on
a makeshift dogsled.
She even tossed him a
dog treat to show her
gratitude.

"Now all I need to

39

do is find my Jeremy!" Candace declared. She strutted off across the snow. Then she stopped short. "Oh, no!" she gasped, her heart sinking. Just ahead of her, Jeremy was chatting with D.D., the Swedish exchange student with the long blond hair. The sun glinted off D.D.'s oversized sunglasses.

"I've got to put a stop to this!" Candace cried. "Oh, Jeremy! Wait! Jeremy!"

Candace started to race toward them, but before she could reach Jeremy, she slipped on a patch of ice—and went sliding across the mountain!

"Why—does—this—keep—happening—to—me?" she screamed as she flew off a cliff and tumbled head over feet down the mountain. At the bottom, she plunged through the frozen surface of a lake, landing in ice-cold water!

Luckily for Candace, a few men were in the middle of an ice-fishing competition. One of them snagged the block of ice with his fishing pole. When he pulled back, he lifted the ice out of the lake—with a shivering Candace frozen inside.

"Too scrawny, throw it back!" the ice-fishing judge ordered.

The fisherman kicked at the ice block, sending it sliding all the way to the ski slopes—right in time for Candace to watch Jeremy and D.D. ski past her.

"Wow, D.D.! You're a really great skier!" Jeremy was saying.

That made Candace so angry, her face turned red. In fact, she was so steamed that her entire body grew hot and melted the ice block around her! She was about to chase after Jeremy when, out of nowhere, Phineas and Ferb zoomed into her on a snowboard.

"Aaaaaaaaaahhh!" Candace screamed as she suddenly found herself riding behind Ferb on the snowboard.

"Hey, Candace!" Phineas exclaimed. "Glad you could join us! This is gonna be great!"

Ferb strapped a helmet onto Candace's

head, and they continued speeding down the mountain!

A moment later, they smashed into a snowman. Now Candace was encased in its body—with a top hat on her head and a carrot in her mouth! She knocked off the hat and spit out the carrot . . . just before the snowboard zoomed through a pine tree. When it emerged on the other side, poor Candace was covered in pine needles from head to foot. She looked like a miniature Christmas tree.

"That's just weird," Phineas said, shaking his head.

The snowboard continued to zip down the mountain, dodging other trees before it reached a ledge.

"Hold on!" Phineas called to Ferb and Candace. The snowboard plunged off the cliff and plummeted in a terrifying free fall! Candace hung on for dear life. When they finally landed on the snow again, she was perched on Ferb's shoulders.

"That's the spirit!" Phineas cheered her on as the snowboard zipped onto a bobsled track and started speeding even faster. The trio raced down the track, dodging other sledders and obstacles before coming upon a giant ski jump.

They launched into the air, sailing higher than they had ever gone before! Suddenly, Phineas realized that Candace was no longer on the back of the snowboard.

"Uh, have you seen Candace?" he asked Ferb.

A scream from under the board caught the boys' attention. They poked their heads over the side and found their sister pressed flat against the bottom of the board, clinging to it with a death grip.

"Oh, hey. Here she is!" Phineas said cheerfully. "You rock, Candace! I didn't even know that was possible!"

Just then, the boys spotted a hot-air balloon

up ahead. Before they could do anything, the snowboard ricocheted off it and plummeted back toward Earth.

"Now this is what I call freestyling!" Phineas yelled into the wind. The three siblings spun wildly, moving faster and faster toward the ground, until they finally crash-landed—right into the snowboarding awards podium. They had won first place! The crowd erupted into thunderous applause.

"Nice!" yelled one kid.

"Totally awesome!" cheered another.

"Wow, that was really cool!" Jeremy said in amazement to Candace as she dismounted.

"Really?" Candace asked.

"You're quite the s'winter athlete," Jeremy said, smiling. "By the way, have you met D.D.?"

Candace narrowed her eyes. "I don't believe I've had the pleasure," she said bitterly.

"Derek Dukenson," the Swedish exchange student said in a heavy accent. Candace stared in surprise as Derek removed his oversized sunglasses. He held out a hand to Candace. "But you can call me D.D."

"Oh!" Candace said in shock. Then she started to giggle. D.D. wasn't a girl after all—just a boy with really long hair! Candace didn't have to worry about D.D. stealing Jeremy away from her. "Nice to meet you, D.D.," she said, very relieved.

Then Candace heard a familiar car horn in the driveway. "Mom and Dad, back already?" she asked in surprise. And Phineas and Ferb's s'winter mountain was still in the backyard. This time, they'd be busted for sure! "This is gonna be the bestest day ever!" she cried.

Candace dashed off to the front yard, still grinning at the thought of what a great day it had turned out to be. She had conquered her fear of heights. And she'd found out that her crush was *not* falling for a gorgeous exchange student. Busting Phineas and Ferb would be the icing on the cake!

There was no way that they could get rid of the enormous snow-covered mountain before Mom and Dad came into the backyard.

Right?

Chapter SIX

Back at the headquarters of Doofenshmirtz Evil, Incorporated, things were not going well for Agent P. Dr. Doofenshmirtz had successfully trapped the secret agent in a pile of sticky string, and he was preparing to fire the Melt-inator 6-5000. Dr. Doofenshmirtz used a remote control to aim the giant laser at the World's Largest Chocolate Bar once more. "You almost foiled my plan!" he said to Agent

P. "Luckily, I had an extra can of sticky string to subdue you with!"

On the floor, Agent P struggled furiously against the pink sticky string that clung to him like a spiderweb. But there was nothing he could do to break free.

Dr. Doofenshmirtz was about to press the ACTIVATE button when suddenly, he paused.

"Whoops, I forgot to plug it in," he said, grabbing an enormous plug and dragging it across the room to an electrical socket. "I always wait until the last minute, because it uses a lot of power!"

Just when all seemed lost, Dr. Doofenshmirtz plugged in the Melt-inator 6-5000 and a blue spark exploded out of the wall, followed by a puff of smoke. Then the power went out!

One by one, streetlights and television sets all over Danville shut down. At the power plant, workers ran around frantically trying to deal with all the flashing lights and ringing alarms. And at Phineas and Ferb's house, all the fans and air conditioners shut down at the same time.

Without the fans to cool it, the towering s'winter mountain began to quickly melt in the

summer heat. It soaked into the ground as if it had never existed.

"Aw, man!" all the kids cried in dismay.

Everyone was thoroughly bummed out, until Isabella called, "Hey, everybody, my mom's got hot chocolate!"

All the kids cheered and started following Isabella to her house.

Meanwhile, Candace was in the front yard grabbing her parents. "Mom! Dad!" she yelled, practically jumping up and down with excitement. "Look at what Phineas and Ferb did to the backyard!"

"Just a second, Candace," her dad grunted as he and her mom struggled to carry the heavy antique cuckoo clock into the house.

"Hurry, hurry! Come on, come on!" Candace cried. "They used a snow-cone machine to build—"

"Do you mind opening the door for us?" her dad interrupted.

Inside the house, Phineas and Ferb's parents carefully hung up their new cuckoo clock.

"Mom, Dad, hurry up!" Candace called as she raced for the backyard and flung open the patio door. "It is a mixture of winter and summer," she said, gesturing outside. "They call it s'winter!"

"I think that'd be wummer, wouldn't it?" her dad asked as they peeked into the yard.

Then Candace's eyes grew wide. She

couldn't believe it. There was no more mountain. All she saw were Phineas and Ferb, licking their snow cones next to a small mound of shaved ice. It was impossible—Phineas and Ferb had gotten away with it again!

Candace's parents shook their heads and headed back into the house while Candace continued to stare openmouthed at the snow-free backyard.

"You know what, Ferb?" Phineas asked his brother once their parents had disappeared into the house. "Today was the best s'winter day ever!" Then he held out his snow cone to his sister. "Last chance, Candace," Phineas said.

Candace took the snow cone, looked at it for a moment, and buried her face in it with a loud *splat*.

Just then, Perry walked by. Now that Dr. Doofenshmirtz's plan was foiled, he had escaped from the silly string and changed back into his disguise as a normal pet platypus.

"Oh, there you are, Perry!" Phineas said happily.

Candace couldn't believe it. She wasn't even able to bust her brothers when they built a giant snow mountain in the backyard! It was like s'winter had never happened. Still, she had gotten to impress Jeremy. So perhaps it wasn't a total loss. And besides, all she had to do was wait until tomorrow. She was sure Phineas and Ferb would have another crazy invention planned. And this time, she would be ready to bust them for sure!

Part
TWO

The doctor smiled at Isabella. "Okay, open your mouth and say 'Ahhhh!'"

Isabella opened her mouth wide. "Ahhhhh!"

Phineas and Ferb stood against the wall. They didn't want to get in the doctor's way. After all, they hadn't come to the hospital for a checkup. They were here to see their good friend Isabella, who had just gotten her tonsils out.

"Oh, good!" Dr. Chong said brightly as she peered into Isabella's open mouth. "The swelling has gone down dramatically!"

Isabella sat back in her hospital bed. She looked a little pale and tired, but otherwise she seemed the same as ever. Especially since she was wearing her Fireside Girls sash with all the badges she'd earned.

"I'll be back to check on you soon," Dr. Chong said as she left.

"So, Isabella, what'cha doin'?" Phineas

asked as he and Ferb approached the bed.

"Oh, just recovering," Isabella replied in a hoarse voice. "But I finally got my tonsillectomy badge!"

"We just came by to cheer you up," Phineas said with a smile.

Isabella pointed to her throat. "Sorry, guys. My throat still hurts like crazy."

Phineas nodded sympathetically. "You know, the best part of getting your tonsils out is that you get to eat all the ice cream you want," he told her.

"Really?" Isabella asked.

"Mountains of it!" Phineas held his arms open wide. "You could have the biggest ice-cream sundae ever made!" Then he snapped his fingers. "Ferb, I know what we're gonna do today!"

Phineas whipped a pencil and pad of paper out of his pocket. "First, we gotta draw up some plans. Wait. No time for that!" He scrawled a note and handed it to Ferb. "You go to Blueprint Heaven. I'll head home to meet the delivery guy." Phineas had a fantastic idea to surprise Isabella, and there wasn't a moment to lose!

As Ferb set off on his mission to Blueprint Heaven, Phineas started dialing a number on his cell phone. "Hello, Blowtorch City?" he said into the phone. "Yeah, I'll hold." Then Phineas looked at Isabella. "When are they letting you out of this joint?"

"This afternoon," Isabella croaked.

"Perfect," Phineas replied with a grin. "We should have just enough time!"

Isabella smiled back. She didn't know exactly *what* Phineas and Ferb were up to, but she'd been friends with the brothers long enough to know that when Phineas got that excited glint in his eyes, he was planning something big.

Maybe even something *huge*!

Meanwhile, in a house high on a hill, Vanessa Doofenshmirtz lounged on a couch. She was dressed all in black, as usual, and flipped casually through the pages of a book.

"So, I'm going out, Vanessa," her mom, Charlene, said from the doorway. "Remember, you're at your dad's this weekend."

Vanessa groaned. "Great, a whole forty-eight hours of evil," she sighed, not bothering to glance up from her book. She was always in a

bad mood when she had to spend the weekend at her father's house. Every time she was there, he was working on some weird, diabolical plot to take over the Tri-State Area.

"Vanessa Doofenshmirtz, your father is not evil," her mom said firmly. "We just didn't get along. We wanted different things."

"Was one of those things to be evil?" asked Vanessa, finally looking up. "Because he's evil!"

"He's not evil, honey," her mom said. "No one's evil."

"No, Mom, he's evil!" Vanessa insisted. She

closed her book and sat up. "You don't know this about him? He has evil schemes! Normal people don't have schemes of any kind. And then there's this secret agent that always bursts in and—"

"I think you're being overly dramatic," her mom interrupted her.

"Mom, I'm not being dramatic," Vanessa said, frustrated. "Dad builds evil contraptions every day. Wait. Let me check on something."

She pulled out her cell phone and dialed her dad's number. Then Vanessa waited for his voice mail to pick up.

"Doofenshmirtz Evil, Incorporated!" the happy jingle played on the other end.

"Yep!" she said. "He's even got his own evil jingle right on his answering machine! Listen!"

Vanessa hit the REDIAL button, then handed the phone to her mother so that she could hear for herself. But this time, Vanessa's dad—Dr. Heinz Doofenshmirtz—answered.

"Hello?" his voice came over the phone.

"Oh, hello, Heinz," Vanessa's mom said.

"Dad!" Vanessa cried, grabbing the phone. "Why'd you pick up? You always let the machine get it!"

"Well, I heard it ring the first time, so I was standing right by the phone," Dr. Doofenshmirtz explained. "Oh, by the way," he added, "could you pick up some blueprints for me on your way over? Thank you, sweetie!" He hung up.

"Great," Vanessa said sarcastically, snapping the cell phone shut. "Now he wants me to pick up some evil blueprints for his latest evil contraption." Suddenly, Vanessa's eyes lit up. "As soon as he's done building it, I'll have proof! I'll call you and you can see for yourself!" she said excitedly to her mother.

Vanessa was so eager to get to Blueprint Heaven that she practically flew out of her mom's house. At last, she had the opportunity to prove that her dad was evil.

This time she would bust him for sure!

Chapter TWO

Nestled in a small building in the heart of downtown Danville, Blueprint Heaven looked like an ordinary store. But just beyond the dingy counter and scuffed floors loomed an inventor's dream: floor-to-ceiling shelves piled high with construction diagrams for everything from rocket ships to roller coasters.

Ferb stood at the counter, waiting patiently for the female clerk to deliver his blueprints.

She frowned a little at the paper note Ferb had handed her.

"So, you need plans to build a giant ice-cream–sundae maker, do ya?" she asked. "Hmmm, I'm not sure we sell blueprints for that anymore."

Ferb blinked.

"Whoa! Hold on, sweetie! No need to get upset!" the clerk exclaimed, throwing her hands into the air. "I'll go check in the back, okay?"

Down an aisle of the warehouse, she climbed a tall ladder. She talked to herself as she searched for the right blueprints. "Okay, let's see. Giant-sundae machine . . ." She called over her shoulder to Ferb, "I've got a yogurt machine. How's that sound?"

Ferb blinked again.

"Yeah, I don't care for yogurt either, baby," the clerk replied. "I'll keep looking."

Just then, the door opened, and in walked Vanessa Doofenshmirtz. She stood next to Ferb at the counter, waiting for her turn.

"You're in luck. I found one!" the clerk said to Ferb as she returned to the counter carrying a rolled-up blueprint in a protective cardboard tube. Then she turned to Vanessa. "Now, what do you need, sweetie?"

"I'm here to pick up an order for Doofenshmirtz," Vanessa replied.

"Oh, yes. Your daddy just called," the clerk said as she shuffled back to the ladder.

Ferb glanced up at the tall, dark-haired girl standing next to him.

"Hey, how's it going?" Vanessa asked him.

Ferb blinked again. She was beautiful!

Meanwhile on the other side of town, Phineas got home from the hospital just before the delivery truck from Blowtorch City arrived. "Can you bring it back here?" he called to the delivery guy. The man slowly started backing the giant truck up into the yard.

Inside the Flynn-Fletcher house, Candace was sprawled across an armchair in the living room. She was chatting with Stacy on the phone. "You're not gonna believe this, Stacy," she said. "But when I turned around, Jeremy was standing right behind me! Well, actually he was sitting and he was a couple of blocks away, but he was right there!"

Outside, Phineas directed the truck. "Keep it coming, keep it coming. Okay, stop! Great! Stack 'em over here!" The delivery man started rolling out a bunch of heavy-looking boxes.

Candace sat up a little straighter when she heard all the commotion. "Um, Stace?" she said into the phone. "I'm gonna have to call you back."

In the yard, the truck driver wheeled a handcart through the grass to deliver the remaining three boxes. "And that's the last of it," he said with a grunt. He turned to Phineas and held out a clipboard. "Just need you to sign right here and . . . say, aren't you a little . . ."

"Young to be using titanium plating and an industrial arc welder?" Phineas finished for him. "Yes. Yes, I am. I get that a lot."

As the driver returned to his truck, Candace stormed up to her brother. "Phineas, you know while Mom's at her cooking class I'm in charge. Now what are you up to out here?" she demanded.

"I'd like to tell you, but it's gonna be a big surprise," Phineas replied. He looked around,

suddenly realizing something. "Hey, wait a second, have you seen Perry?"

Over on the other side of the yard, out of sight of the siblings, their pet platypus, Perry, was curled up on a bright green patch of grass for an afternoon nap in the sunshine.

Sproing!

Without warning, a giant spring launched the patch of grass out of the ground and sent Perry soaring high into the air! The

platypus landed right in a waiting hoverjet, and his fedora fell onto his head just in time to transform him into Agent P! Now wide awake, he zoomed off through the sky. A moment later, an urgent message from Major Monogram appeared on the hoverjet's video screen.

"Sorry to wake you, Agent P," Major Monogram apologized. "Looks like Doofenshmirtz is getting sloppy. He sent his daughter right into our sting operation and purchased blueprints for a Space-Laser-inator."

Major Monogram paused as a picture of Vanessa flashed onto the screen. Then the camera zoomed out, revealing that Major Monogram was standing in the middle of Blueprint Heaven. "We intended to pass him fake plans, but due to a rookie error . . . and by 'rookie,' I mean Carl—"

Major Monogram glared as his intern, Carl, also appeared on-screen—dressed as the female clerk from Blueprint Heaven.

"Sorry. My bad," Carl apologized.

"The plans he received are real," Major

Monogram continued. "Terrifyingly real!"

"Again, I must apologize," Carl said. "I was in character and—"

"You'd better step on it, Agent P, before it's too late!" Major Monogram said.

Agent P saluted at the monitor and gunned the engine. He was headed straight for the headquarters of Doofenshmirtz Evil, Incorporated. And he knew that there wasn't a moment to lose!

In the Flynn-Fletcher backyard, Phineas juggled three big boxes in his arms. They were piled high, and he didn't want to risk dropping one. "Can you give me a hand unpacking this stuff, Candace?" he asked.

Candace frowned and put her hands on her hips. "I'm not going to help you, but as soon as I figure out what you're up to, I'm calling Mom!" she snapped.

"Okay," Phineas replied in a friendly voice as he started to walk across the lawn. "Say hi for me!"

The minute Phineas was out of earshot, Candace whipped out her phone and dialed her mother. Mrs. Flynn-Fletcher was just about to begin her cooking class at Chef Guilbaud's culinary school.

"Bonjour, class!" Chef Guilbaud announced in a French accent at the front of the room. "Today, we'll be making crêpes Guilbaud."

Just then, Mrs. Flynn-Fletcher's cell phone started ringing loudly! She grabbed it before it could ring again. "Candace, is everything all right?" she said quietly into the phone. On the other end, Candace explained that Phineas was up to something, but she didn't know what. "Well, if you don't even know what he's doing, how do you know if it's a problem?" her mom replied, annoyed.

At the front of the classroom, Chef Guilbaud

cleared his throat loudly. *"Ahem.* Is there something you would like to share with the whole class?" he asked.

"Sorry, sir," Candace's mom said at once. Then she whispered into the phone, "Candace, I'll talk to you later, okay?"

"Argh," Candace growled when her mom hung up. She pointed her finger at Phineas. "I'm keeping an eye on you!"

Candace stormed off just as Ferb got home from Blueprint Heaven.

"Hey, Ferb, you got the blueprints?" Phineas asked. Ferb handed him the rolled-up plans.

"Excellent!" Phineas said. "Isabella's gonna love it!"

With the supplies from Blowtorch City and the plans from Blueprint Heaven, Phineas and Ferb had everything they needed to build the biggest ice-cream–sundae maker ever. Phineas couldn't think of a nicer way to welcome Isabella home from the hospital— especially since she had just had her tonsils out.

But the brothers had to hurry, because she would be home in just a few hours. Phineas wanted to make sure they were ready to greet her with the most amazing ice-cream sundae in the world!

Meanwhile, across town, Agent P expertly landed his hoverjet on the balcony of Doofenshmirtz Evil, Incorporated. Then he banged open the front door with a swift karate kick!

"Perry the Platypus, you're early!" Dr. Doofenshmirtz exclaimed in surprise. The evil doctor was surrounded by open boxes overflowing with all sorts of strange and sinister-looking metal parts. "I haven't even started yet. My daughter should be here any minute with the blueprints, though."

As if on cue, Vanessa strolled through the front door, carrying a set of diagrams in a cardboard tube. She gave Agent P a curious look as she entered.

"Oh, there she is," said Dr. Doofenshmirtz. "Good morning, Vanessa. You remember Perry the Platypus?"

"Yeah," Vanessa said flatly. "Hi."

"Perry the Platypus, why don't you have a seat in my waiting area?" Dr. Doofenshmirtz offered, pointing to a lobby filled with comfy chairs, games, and even children's toys. "Read some magazines. Sorry they're all in Spanish. I steal them from my neighbor. You know, evil never rests."

As Agent P sat down and started flipping through a magazine, Vanessa followed her father into his lair. "So, Dad, this plan . . . it's evil, right?" she said, trying to sound casual.

"Oh, yes!" Dr. Doofenshmirtz assured her. "Yes, it is! It's nice to see you taking an interest in the family business."

"That's all I need to know," Vanessa replied. Smiling smugly, she dialed her mom's cell phone number.

Once more, a phone rang at Chef Guilbaud's cooking school. But this time it was Vanessa's mom who got the call.

"I'm in class now, Vanessa," her mom said quietly into the phone. "I have to go." She paused as Vanessa explained something on the other end. "Mmm-hmm. Mmm-hmm. Yes, Vanessa, I'll leave my phone on," she assured her daughter.

As she hung up, Vanessa's mom turned

to Mrs. Flynn-Fletcher, who was sharing a cooking station with her. "Teenagers. Ugh!" She shrugged.

Mrs. Flynn-Fletcher nodded in agreement. If there was one thing that she understood, it was how frustrating it could be to have a teenage daughter who always wanted to get someone else in trouble!

Chapter
FOUR

All afternoon, Vanessa took careful notes as Dr. Doofenshmirtz assembled his latest contraption. Her father was following the blueprints precisely as they were written. Little did Vanessa know that across town, at the Flynn-Fletcher house, Candace was spying on Phineas and Ferb in the exact same way. Both girls were determined to do some busting—no matter what!

At last, Dr. Doofenshmirtz was finished. "Oh, Perry the Platypus!" he called out. "It's finally ready!"

Agent P glanced up from his magazine. But before he could get out of his chair, Dr. Doofenshmirtz pushed a large orange button on the wall. In an instant, the chair spun around and a tiny steel cage popped out! The metal bars knocked off Agent P's fedora as they closed around him. He was trapped! A robotic claw whisked the platypus over to Dr. Doofenshmirtz.

"Too bad you can do nothing but watch as

I prepare to launch my Space-Laser-inator!"
Dr. Doofenshmirtz cackled with glee. From
beneath a large sheet, he revealed a giant
machine made of silvery steel with blue-tinted
panels and a revolving radar antenna on
top. Four valves released ominous plumes of
smoke.

"Wow, I bet that thing must be really evil,
huh?" Vanessa asked with wide eyes.

Dr. Doofenshmirtz smiled proudly at his
daughter. "Vanessa, take a look out that

window and tell me what you see," he said.

Vanessa walked past the Space-Laser-inator and stared out the window. But she couldn't see anything because a giant billboard was blocking the view. "Uh . . . not much," she replied.

"Exactly!" cried Dr. Doofenshmirtz. "Ever since that stupid billboard went up, my panoramic view has been completely ruined! I used to have this perfect vantage point for enjoying the delicious misery of others," he said, remembering all the car wrecks in the busy intersection below that he used to be able to watch from his window.

"But after I launch this baby into orbit, my problem will be solved," he explained. His Space-Laser-inator would blast the billboard apart! "Then I can go on to eliminate all the other annoyances that make my skin crawl. Like, uh, nature! Beauty! And even morning talk-show hosts! Soon there will be nothing that can withstand the wrath of Dr. Heinz Doofenshmirtz!"

"Doctor?" Vanessa interrupted. "Since when are you a doctor?"

Dr. Doofenshmirtz grabbed his diploma to show her. "They don't just give these out to anybody, you know!"

Vanessa noticed a price tag hanging off the diploma. "Anybody with fifteen bucks they do," she said.

"That's enough looking!" Dr. Doofenshmirtz snatched the frame away from her. "I'd love to debate you, but I have some pressing business to take care of—like remaking the Tri-State Area in my own twisted image!"

"Oh, my gosh!" Vanessa exclaimed as her dad went over to operate the machine. "This is worse than I thought!" She started frantically dialing her mom's cell phone number. "Oh! Dad is gonna be so busted!" She grinned.

Meanwhile, at the Chef Guilbaud cooking school, Vanessa's mom and Mrs. Flynn-Fletcher were just pouring the batter for their crêpes when . . .

Brrrriiinnnggg!

Charlene's cell phone went off and she dropped the pitcher. Glass and crêpe mix splattered everywhere!

"Oh, for Pete's sake!" Vanessa's mom cried as she grabbed her phone. "Vanessa?"

Then Mrs. Flynn-Fletcher's cell rang, too.

"Candace?" she asked as she answered it. "This had better be important."

"He's doing what?" Vanessa's mom said into the phone.

"Honey, are you sure you're not exaggerating just a little bit?" Candace's mom asked.

"Well, I—it's not that I don't believe you, honey . . ." Vanessa's mom continued.

"Every time I race home, I find out everything is just fine!" Candace's mom said.

"Yes, I'll be right over," Vanessa's mom sighed.

"I'm on my way," Candace's mom said. She snapped her cell phone shut and shrugged. "Teenagers."

"Tell me about it." Vanessa's mom nodded.

Both women hurried off, leaving their unfinished crêpes burning on the stove.

Meanwhile, Candace and Vanessa both smiled as they hung up their phones. Their busting plans seemed foolproof.

What could possibly go wrong?

At last, the moment he'd been waiting for had arrived. With a remote control in hand, Dr. Doofenshmirtz was prepared to unleash the all powerful Space-Laser-inator on the city of Danville! "Now, to launch my creation and begin my reign of evil terror!" he cackled.

Agent P struggled against the cage, but it was no use. He was still trapped. Dr. Doofenshmirtz flipped the switch, and a high-pitched whirring noise filled his lair. The Space-Laser-inator started to rumble and shake. Dr. Doofenshmirtz rubbed his hands together with glee. But then, an enormous silver spoon suddenly shot out from one side of the machine, scooping up Dr. Doofenshmirtz and holding him beneath a spout that had also popped out.

Dr. Doofenshmirtz looked up in confusion. There hadn't been anything like *this* in the plans. But before he could scramble out of the spoon—s*plat*!

An enormous mound of frosty mint-chocolate-chip ice cream squirted all over him!

Then, *plunk*!

A huge cherry landed right on his head!

"Blech. Well, this can't be right!" cried Dr. Doofenshmirtz.

Meanwhile, on the other side of town, Phineas and Ferb had just finished building their own contraption. They placed a fancy glass dish under the machine, ready for it to catch a delicious scoop of ice cream.

"Get ready for a giant sundae!" Phineas said excitedly as he pressed the START button. The machine began to shake and sputter. The ground trembled. Then, to the brothers' surprise, rocket jets erupted from the bottom of the machine, and it blasted off into the sky!

"Well, this can't be right." Phineas frowned. "Let me see those blueprints." Ferb handed him the plans. "Oh, wait a minute," Phineas said. "These are the plans for a Space-Laser-inator, apparently. I was wondering what that thing was for." Phineas pointed in the direction of a scary-looking laser gun made out of black metal. "It's a good thing we didn't attach it, huh?" he said to his stepbrother.

Suddenly, the boys heard a commotion on the patio. "Mom! Mom! Hurry! Come on! Come on!" It was Candace, calling loudly to the boys' mother as she ran into the backyard. Candace pointed excitedly at Phineas and Ferb.

"Hi, kids. How are you doing?" their mom asked.

"We're just about to make a nice handmade sundae for Isabella," Phineas replied as Ferb picked up the large ice-cream dish.

"Huh?" Candace asked in bewilderment.

"Oh, that is so sweet!" their mom said. "Come on in the kitchen, I'll help you with it."

At the same time, Vanessa and her mother were riding in an elevator up to the top floor of Doofenshmirtz Evil, Incorporated. "Come on, Mom! Hurry!" Vanessa cried as she dragged her mother out of the elevator and down the hallway. She pointed to her father. "See? Evil! I told you!" she cried.

Her mom stepped through the doorway and took a long look at her ex-husband, covered in ice cream and with a cherry on top of his head. "Hmm," she said. "Uh, that's not evil, dear. A bit much, perhaps. Heinz, what is all this? I thought you were lactose intolerant?"

"I am!" Dr. Doofenshmirtz whined.

Vanessa's mom frowned as she picked up the remote and flipped the switch. The machine squirted another enormous heap of ice cream onto Dr. Doofenshmirtz!

"And what's that over there?" Vanessa's mom asked, pointing to Perry inside the cage. "That is no way to treat your pet!"

She marched across the room and gently lifted Perry out of the cage.

"But, Mom! That's the secret agent!" Vanessa cried as she rushed over.

"A secret agent?" her mom said, raising an eyebrow. "He's just a little platypus. They don't do much, you know."

Vanessa scowled. It was clear her mom just wasn't getting an evil vibe from the ridiculous scene at Doofenshmirtz Evil, Incorporated.

But Vanessa knew her dad pretty well, and she guessed that it was only a matter of time before he launched yet another evil scheme. And when he did, she would be ready to bust him, if it was the last thing she did!

* * *

A short while later, Phineas and Ferb went over to Isabella's house to deliver a very special treat: the ice-cream sundae that their mom had helped them make. With three scoops of ice cream, hot-fudge sauce, whipped cream, two cookies, and a juicy cherry on top, it looked absolutely delicious!

"Wow, guys!" Isabella said. She still sounded pretty hoarse, but she was looking much happier. "This is amazing! I was afraid you guys were going to go overboard and build some giant sundae contraption or something."

"Actually, we were gonna do that." Phineas shrugged. "But we accidentally built a space laser instead." Then he turned to his brother. "Ferb, you're usually so focused. How'd you get those blueprints confused?"

Ferb blinked. He thought back to how he had been standing at the counter of Blueprint Heaven. And he remembered when the tall, dark-haired, gorgeous girl had walked in. It was a moment he'd never forget, a moment when he could practically hear music playing and see flowers falling from above.

"Hey," Vanessa had said in the most beautiful voice he had ever heard. "How's it going?"

"Hey, Ferb!" Phineas said, giving his stepbrother a shake. "Snap out of it. What happened back there?"

Ferb blinked again before finally admitting, "I was weak."

Phineas looked at his stepbrother in confusion. He wasn't sure he'd ever truly understand

what had happened at Blueprint Heaven. But it was okay. After all, Isabella's sundae turned out just right, even without the giant ice-cream maker. And tomorrow, another summer day would begin—which meant that Phineas and Ferb would have another chance to make it the best day ever!

Don't miss the fun in the next

Phineas & Ferb book...

Journey to Mars

Adapted by Ellie O'Ryan

Based on the series created by Dan Povenmire & Jeff "Swampy" Marsh

Phineas and Ferb were sprawled under a tree in their backyard as sunlight streamed through the leaves overhead. It was another fun day of summer vacation, and all the boys had to do was figure out how to spend it!

Ever since they had vowed to have the best summer ever, Phineas and Ferb's days had been filled with one adventure after another. Phineas and Ferb weren't just stepbrothers— they were also best friends! And from Phineas's nonstop ideas to Ferb's exceptional building skills, they made a great team . . . especially when it came time to plan each day's activities. In fact, Phineas and Ferb had so many excellent ideas they'd started to keep track of them all in a list on their laptop.

"What should we do today?" Phineas asked as he scrolled through the list. "Build an underwater skate park? Sounds pretty wicked! Fly with rocket-powered bat wings? Awesome! Teach Perry tricks?"

Phineas paused to look down at his pet platypus, Perry, who was perched nearby. "He's just a platypus. He doesn't do much," Phineas said, shrugging his shoulders.

Perry started chattering in response, making a cute little platypus noise that seemed to confirm what Phineas had said. But in reality, Perry was a secret operative known as Agent P! He worked for O.W.C.A., or Organization Without a Cool Acronym. O.W.C.A. was dedicated to identifying and fighting evil in all its forms, and because of the sensitive nature of these secret activities, O.W.C.A. agents went deep undercover. Years of training had turned Agent P into one of the smartest, most skilled platypuses on the planet—but only a few people in the world knew that. And to protect Agent P's secret identity, Phineas and Ferb were not among them.

Before Phineas could get back to reading through his list, a visitor arrived in the backyard. It was Isabella Garcia-Shapiro, leader of the local Fireside Girls troop and one of Phineas's and Ferb's best friends and neighbors!

"Oh, hi, Isabella!" Phineas exclaimed.

"Hey, Phineas, you might want to go check up on Baljeet," Isabella said with a worried look on her face. "I was walking by his house and heard him scream, 'Ay-eee! I'm doomed to be an incompetent flunky forever . . . ever . . . ever . . . ever . . .'" Isabella let her voice trail off. "I added the echo part," she said.

Phineas and Ferb were already on their feet, and Perry jumped up, too. "Sounds pretty serious," Phineas said as he grabbed his computer. Then he and Ferb hurried out to the sidewalk, thinking Perry was trailing behind them. But they were wrong. Perry had important spy business to attend to.

Their friend Baljeet Rai lived just a few blocks away. "Baljeet! It's Phineas and Ferb!" Phineas called as he and Ferb walked into Baljeet's house. They hurried down the hall to his bedroom, which was dark and gloomy. "Why are all the lights off?" Phineas asked.

Sitting in the shadows, Baljeet didn't even look up. "Darkness is a shroud that hides my shame," he said sadly. Then he buried his face in his hands.

"Hey, buddy. Why don't you tell us what's going on?" Phineas asked with concern.

"Because of the seventeen summer school classes I am taking, I qualified for the science fair," Baljeet explained. He unrolled a stack of papers. "So, I decided to design this."

Phineas and Ferb glanced at the papers and realized that they were blueprints. "A portal to Mars? Cool!" Phineas exclaimed.

"No! Not cool," Baljeet replied, grabbing the blueprints and rolling them back up. "When I showed my teacher, he said . . ." Baljeet closed his eyes at the memory. He could still hear the disbelief in Mr. McGillicuddy's voice when he asked, "A portal to Mars? And . . . what does it do?"

"Well, without overcomplicating things, it's a . . . portal to Mars," Baljeet told his teacher. "You step through it, and you're on Mars."